This Barbie Annual belongs to

....

My age ....

Written by Jane Clempner
Designed by Sheryl Bone

Published in Great Britain in 2004 by
Egmont Books Limited, 239 Kensington High Street, London, W8 6SA.
Printed in Dubai

ISBN: 1 4052 1391 4

This is your special Barbie
Annual, so fill in your name!

WELCOME to the most magical Barbie Annual ever! It's bursting with fashion, stories and fun things to do. Turn the pages and travel with Barbie from a winter wonderland... to an enchanted forest!
When you're in Barbie Town, magic really can happen!

BARBIE™

just remember - think pink!

Contents

Girls, wanna have fun?
Then you're in the right place! Pink it up!
Barbie X

Frosty Flurry

BARBIE™

Follow the Barbie trail to a
winter wonderland...

7

The Snow Dome

"Bobble hat and boots."

"Check."

"Sunglasses."

"Check."

"Pink gloves, pink jacket, pink passport?"

"Check." Barbie put the list down.

"What's wrong?" asked Kira. "You're jetting off to France for a week's skiing while I'm stuck here. I should have the long face!"

"Sorry," Barbie shrugged. "I wish you were coming. My relatives are all so old! It's going to be *so* dull."

"Dull?" shrieked Kira. "Just packing your suitcase makes *me* feel excited!"

Barbie looked down at her pink skis and tried to smile…

8

STORY

"You're jetting off to France for a week's skiing!"

Four hours later, Barbie wheeled the same skis from the airport in Geneva and followed her relatives onto the minibus.

Next thing she knew, she was stepping down in a mountain village. She blinked her sleepy eyes and reached for her sunglasses, then stood on the snowy ground and stared.

The village was made of sugar icing! People were gliding on soft, silent skis and, up above, the sun shone from a wide dome of blue. Barbie gazed at the distant slopes peppered with skiers and felt a tingle of excitement.

Barbie gazed at the distant slopes and felt a tingle of excitement.

The next morning, dressed in her matching salopettes, jacket and gloves, with her lift pass dangling around her neck, she arrived at ski school. But it was not quite as she expected.

"I can't stay here with all these … babies!" she said, looking in horror at the little children in her group. Her instructor was too busy to argue, so Barbie headed for the nearest ski-lift and glided to the top of the mountain. She breathed in the clean air and felt the warmth of the sun, which shone dazzlingly on the untouched snow.

Barbie dismounted at the top of the mountain and was quite alone. She stood and stared at the beautiful white wonderland for a long time … too long, as suddenly she realised the sun was sinking, taking its warmth with it.

She felt cold – freezing in fact. The sky went grey, then black. A wind picked up and stirred the freezing snow, which blew icily into her face.

STORY

"I can't stay here with all these … babies!"

She called out – but there was no one to hear. And now Barbie remembered – she couldn't ski!

Suddenly a figure on a snowboard appeared. "Keep your knees bent and your skis straight," he ordered in a strong French accent. And, taking hold of her waist firmly, he guided her safely down the mountain.

Inside a warm and welcoming café, Barbie sat shakily on a stool at the bar, while her rescuer ordered two hot chocolates.
"Voilà!" he said, passing her a steaming mug and taking off his hat and goggles. Barbie stared at his brown eyes, tanned skin and spiky black hair. He was so handsome!
"S'il vous plaît, drink your chocolat, you are lucky to be alive!" he said.
His accent made Barbie giggle.

Barbie stared at his brown eyes, tanned skin and spiky black hair. He was so handsome!

"It is not for laughing!" he said, crossly. "The snow is full of danger … " He looked around and picked up a pretty glass snow dome from the bar. "One minute quiet and the next … " He shook the snow dome. "Regardez! Un blizzard!" Now Barbie blushed. She was feeling more flustered than she could ever remember.

"You *must* learn to ski; it is très, très important!"
"I … I will. I'm sorry … "
"Tomorrow you must go to ski school." He stood up to leave.
"Please … what is your name? Will I see you again?" she asked, blushing even more.
He took hold of her hand. "Je m'appelle Laurent. I teach snowboarding. I will see you … soon."

The following morning, Barbie went to ski school. She went the next morning and afternoon and every day after that. She soon became a star pupil, and moved quickly from the nursery slopes to the green runs. Every day she hoped to see Laurent, but he never came. On the final day, her instructor said she was ready to tackle the pink run.

Pink ◆

STORY

"You must learn to ski; it is très, très important!"

Standing at the top of the long slope, her legs felt like jelly. But she really wanted to do this. She lowered her goggles and pushed off.

And there, at the foot of the mountain, waiting to greet her with a dazzling smile, was Laurent!

Arm in arm, they went to their café and ordered hot chocolates. But this time Laurent did not hurry to leave. They sat in armchairs by the fire and talked and laughed until the world outside grew dark and the dome of sky above them glittered with stars.

The next morning, as Barbie settled into her seat on the plane, she felt like crying. She shivered and pulled her coat tightly around her.

Arm in arm, they went to their café and ordered hot chocolates.

STORY

13

There was something in one of her pockets. She reached in and pulled out the glass snow dome. Laurent must have put it there. She smiled and shook it gently. The snow inside fluttered like the feelings in her heart. At the same moment, as the plane took off, somewhere on the white slopes Laurent shivered too. If Barbie had looked down she might have seen the heart he had drawn in the snow.

And who knows, maybe love will make their paths cross again, one day …

14

She reached in and pulled out the glass snow dome.

Puzzle Fun!

Laurent has written a coded message on the ice. Can you work out what it says?

PUZZLE

Here are nine snow domes.
Which two are identical?

Colour Barbie in her
romantic winter wonderland.

17

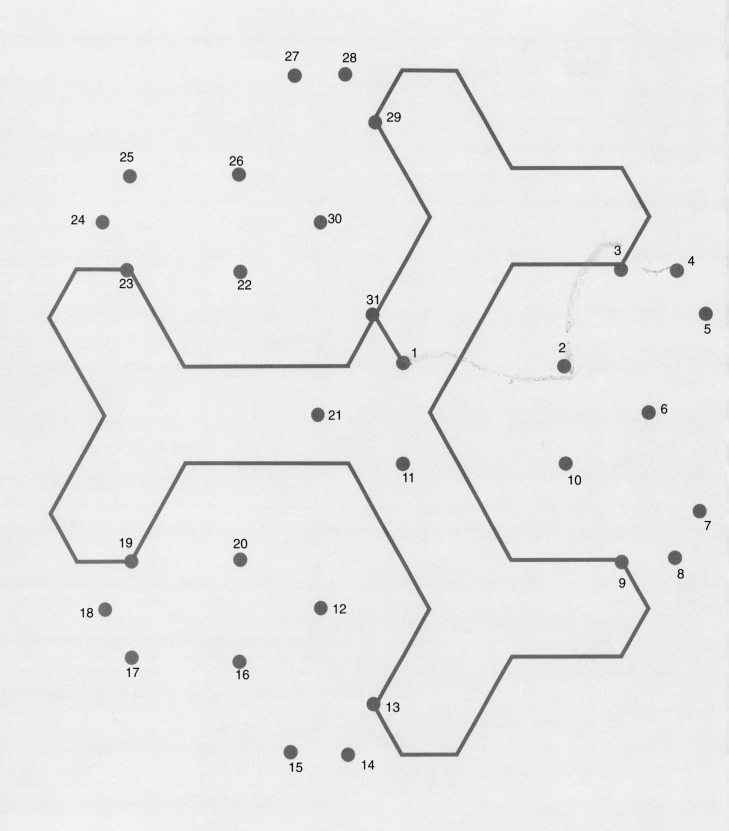

27 28

29

25 26

24 30 3 4

23 22 31 5

1 2

21 6

11 10

7

19 20 9 8

18

17 16 12 13

15 14

PUZZLE

Snowflakes are beautiful and come in all shapes and sizes. Join the dots in the correct order to finish this one.

Barbie and her friends just wanna
have fun ...

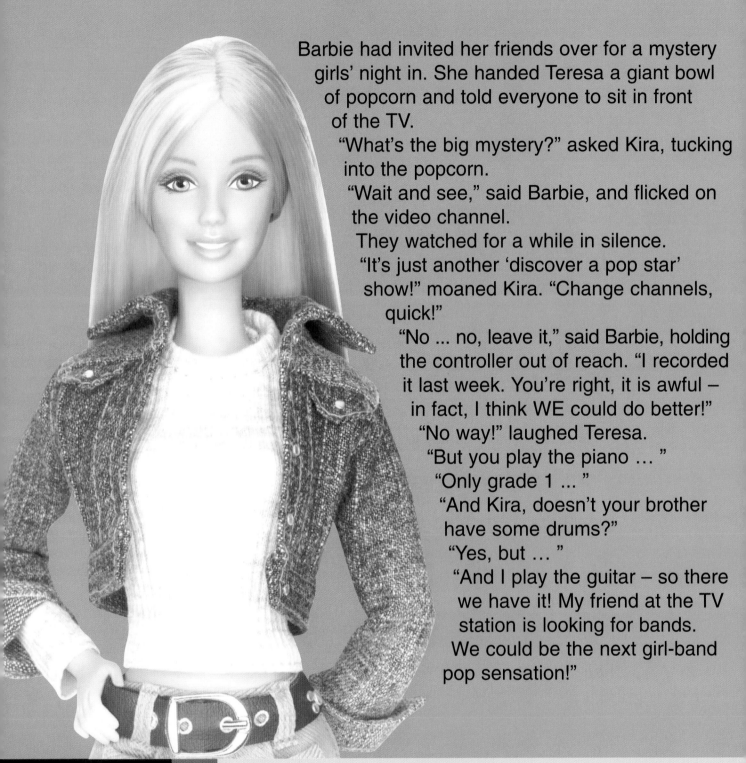

Barbie had invited her friends over for a mystery girls' night in. She handed Teresa a giant bowl of popcorn and told everyone to sit in front of the TV.

"What's the big mystery?" asked Kira, tucking into the popcorn.

"Wait and see," said Barbie, and flicked on the video channel.

They watched for a while in silence.

"It's just another 'discover a pop star' show!" moaned Kira. "Change channels, quick!"

"No ... no, leave it," said Barbie, holding the controller out of reach. "I recorded it last week. You're right, it is awful – in fact, I think WE could do better!"

"No way!" laughed Teresa.

"But you play the piano ... "

"Only grade 1 ... "

"And Kira, doesn't your brother have some drums?"

"Yes, but ... "

"And I play the guitar – so there we have it! My friend at the TV station is looking for bands. We could be the next girl-band pop sensation!"

20

STORY

"And Kira, doesn't your brother have some drums?"

Barbie leapt to her feet and sent the popcorn tumbling across the floor. "Just imagine being whisked off to the airport in a limo and having a team of people to dress us and bring us milkshakes any time of the day!"

"Um … reality check!" laughed Teresa. "Grade 1 piano does not equal pop star."

"And we can't sing!" added Kira.

"Where's your sense of adventure?" asked Barbie. She grabbed a hairbrush from the floor and held it like a microphone. "Put your hands together for those sensational girls with attitude – the Pink Dolls!!!" She made a noise like applause. "I can see it now … our first single will top the charts and our album will go multi-platinum!"

Teresa looked at Kira and spiralled her finger at the side of her head. "Barbie's gone mad!"

"You're right!" said Barbie, sitting down again. "Not about me being mad, but that none of us can sing!"

But that wasn't going to stop her!

Two days later, in the garage, the Pink Dolls met for their first rehearsal. Barbie rushed in, waving a large poster.

"None of us can sing!"

"How's this?" she asked, holding it up for all to see. "We'll put it up in the common room at school."

ARE YOU A SINGER WAITING TO BE DISCOVERED? DO YOU HAVE WHAT IT TAKES TO BE A STAR?

Then join the next pop sensation

The Pink Dolls™

Contact BARBIE for more details

The following Friday, in the garage, the Pink Dolls sat behind a decorating table, notepads at the ready. Outside, the nervous singers formed a short queue. Barbie called them in, one by one.
After ten minutes, all four singers had gone home. Barbie picked up her notepad and flicked through the pages. "Useless … dreadful … eeeek … looks good but can't sing … I give up!"

STORY

The nervous singers formed a short queue.

But, just as they began packing away, a face appeared around the garage door.

"Hi … am I too late?"

Barbie glanced up at the pretty, red-haired girl standing in the doorway. She had a guitar over her shoulder.

"No … come in, please. Are you going to sing?" asked Barbie, her spirits lifted.

"Yes … my name's Sophie. And this is one of my songs … "

As the first notes filled the empty garage, Barbie felt her skin tingle. The panel listened in silence and, as the song finished and the beautiful voice faded away, Barbie had to clear her throat before she could speak.

"Um ... oh my goodness. You sing amazingly!" She looked at the others. "I think I speak for everyone when I say – welcome to the Pink Dolls!"

Rehearsals took place in the garage every Friday after school.

As the first notes filled the empty garage, Barbie felt her skin tingle.

STORY

23

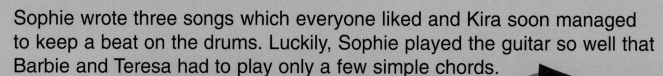

Sophie wrote three songs which everyone liked and Kira soon managed to keep a beat on the drums. Luckily, Sophie played the guitar so well that Barbie and Teresa had to play only a few simple chords.
Six weeks later, they had a demo tape ready to send to the TV station.

For a week they heard nothing. Then Barbie had a phone call. She called an emergency meeting in the garage.
"There's no easy way to say this, so I'll just say it," she began. "They think we're rubbish." She waited for a reaction.
"We knew that anyway," smiled Kira.
"But," continued Barbie, "they think our singer is amazing and a record company wants to sign her up!" All four girls leapt up and began squealing with excitement.
"We knew that too!" laughed Barbie. "You *are* amazing, Sophie. And the Pink Dolls will go on without you!"
"Or not," corrected Kira. "My dad wants his garage back, and my brother's selling his drums."

STORY

24

"There's no easy way to say this ...
they think we're rubbish."

"Oh well, it was fun while it lasted!" smiled Barbie. "And you'd better mention us on your first CD, Sophie."
"And invite us backstage at your first concert!"
And you know, she did.

"Invite us backstage at your first concert!"

STORY

25

Pink It Up!

If you were in a band, what would you like to be called?
Write your band's name here.

....

Who would you choose to join your band?

....

....

....

Which instruments would you play?

....

....

And who would be the singer?

....

Make up a title for your first song!

....

ACTIVITY

Fill in the answers above to
create your own dream band.

Colour the Pink Dolls to make them look like stars.

PUZZLE

Which of the five silhouettes matches the guitarist exactly?

Draw a line to join these funky guitars into pairs.

Are You a Future Star?

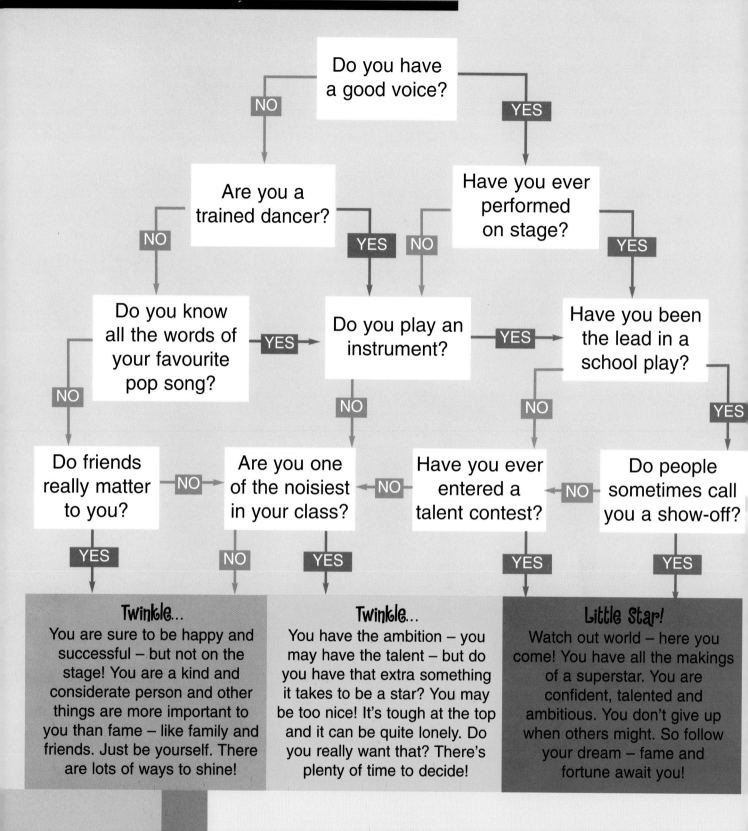

Do you have a good voice?

NO → **Are you a trained dancer?**

YES → **Have you ever performed on stage?**

Are you a trained dancer?
- NO → **Do you know all the words of your favourite pop song?**
- YES → **Do you play an instrument?**

Have you ever performed on stage?
- NO → **Do you play an instrument?**
- YES → **Have you been the lead in a school play?**

Do you know all the words of your favourite pop song?
- NO → **Do friends really matter to you?**
- YES → **Do you play an instrument?**

Do you play an instrument?
- NO → **Are you one of the noisiest in your class?**
- YES → **Have you been the lead in a school play?**

Have you been the lead in a school play?
- NO → **Do people sometimes call you a show-off?**
- YES → **Do people sometimes call you a show-off?**

Do friends really matter to you?
- NO → **Are you one of the noisiest in your class?**
- YES → Twinkle...

Are you one of the noisiest in your class?
- NO → Twinkle...
- YES → Twinkle...

Have you ever entered a talent contest?
- NO → **Are you one of the noisiest in your class?**
- YES → Twinkle...

Do people sometimes call you a show-off?
- NO → **Have you ever entered a talent contest?**
- YES → Little Star!

Twinkle...
You are sure to be happy and successful – but not on the stage! You are a kind and considerate person and other things are more important to you than fame – like family and friends. Just be yourself. There are lots of ways to shine!

Twinkle...
You have the ambition – you may have the talent – but do you have that extra something it takes to be a star? You may be too nice! It's tough at the top and it can be quite lonely. Do you really want that? There's plenty of time to decide!

Little Star!
Watch out world – here you come! You have all the makings of a superstar. You are confident, talented and ambitious. You don't give up when others might. So follow your dream – fame and fortune await you!

Quiz

Have fun with this quiz to find out if you might be the next singing sensation!

It's time for Barbie to choose
her top ten special things ...

is off to Barbie Town University, but she really doesn't want to leave her friends!

Kira and Teresa come over to help her pack. They choose her outfit – a funky , cute , blue and hip .

But has too many other clothes to fit in her !

"Choose your top 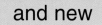 favourite outfits and put those in your ," suggests Kira.

"There's no room for my best and new !" cries . "And what about my ! I can't live without those!"

"We'll bring them when we visit," says Teresa.

"I'll when I arrive," sighs .

"And to us about all the fun stuff you do," adds Kira.

"I 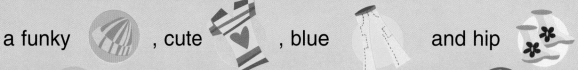 you guys," says . "You two are top of my list of

Special Things™."

STORY

Swap the pictures for words and read the story out loud.

1.

2.

3.

4.

5.

6.

7.

8.

9.

10.

Make a list of your top ten special things
- you can include your best friends!

ACTIVITY

33

Here's the bedroom Barbie has at home – and her new bedroom at university! They are very similar!

PUZZLE

But can you spot ten differences between them?

Colour Barbie in her new Barbie Town
University look. Doesn't she look grown up?

The Poochie Parlour is the most happening place in Barbie Town ...

There was excitement in Barbie Town. "Come to this year's Pet Show … " Teresa was reading the notice that had appeared in the window of the Poochie Parlour. "Meet this year's special guest judge … Jason from the TV show, Perfect Pets!"

"Wow!" gasped Kira. "I'm going to enter my goldfish, just to get a look at Jason – he's scrummy!"

"We should all enter," added Teresa. "It'll be fun!"

Just then, the door to the Poochie Parlour opened and out walked a tall, rather serious-looking girl, carrying a beautifully groomed cat. The girls went silent until she had gone.

"Oh," sighed Teresa. "We all forgot about Pru and her Persian Princess. She wins every year. That miserable cat is more pampered than a top model!"

"And Pru always looks down her nose at everyone," agreed Barbie. "Anyway, I don't think my dog, Muffin, stands a chance! I love him to bits, but he hates the sight of water. He'd never stay still long enough to be groomed!"

"Pru always looks down her nose at everyone!"

The following Saturday, Barbie took Muffin to the park. He loved chasing his squeaky ball, leaping over bushes, round flowerbeds and through swings to catch it. But after ten minutes, he was caked in mud and brambles.

Barbie scooped him up. "There's only one place for you," she said, and headed straight for the Poochie Parlour. Inside, she couldn't quite believe her eyes. Cats were sitting happily under hairdryers; dogs were quietly being washed and not making a fuss; and there at the grooming table was Pru. Persian Princess was purring loudly as the assistant clipped her claws!

Pru looked towards Barbie.
Barbie smiled.
Pru sniffed haughtily and Muffin chose that precise moment to catch sight of the soapy water. He leapt down and raced out of the shop, knocking over a stand of diamanté dog collars on the way. Barbie blushed and ran after him.

38

He leapt down and raced out of the shop.

She never wanted to go there again. In fact, she forgot all about the Pet Show until she was walking through Barbie Town the following week and noticed the marquee. She didn't like to give in – at least not without trying!

And so, on the morning of the Pet Show, she took Muffin to her bedroom. He looked scruffier than ever. She knew he hated water, but at the back of the bathroom cabinet she found a sachet of dry shampoo. She sprinkled it all over his coat and then blasted him with her hairdryer. At first it seemed to be working. He looked quite clean and fluffy, but then, to her horror, his coat started to turn blue and stand up on end! Barbie checked the sachet. It was her grandma's blue hair dye! Poor Muffin now looked like a big blue ball of wool. He looked up at her with pleading eyes.
"I still love you!" she said. "Come on, we'll show them!"

To her horror, his coat started to turn blue!

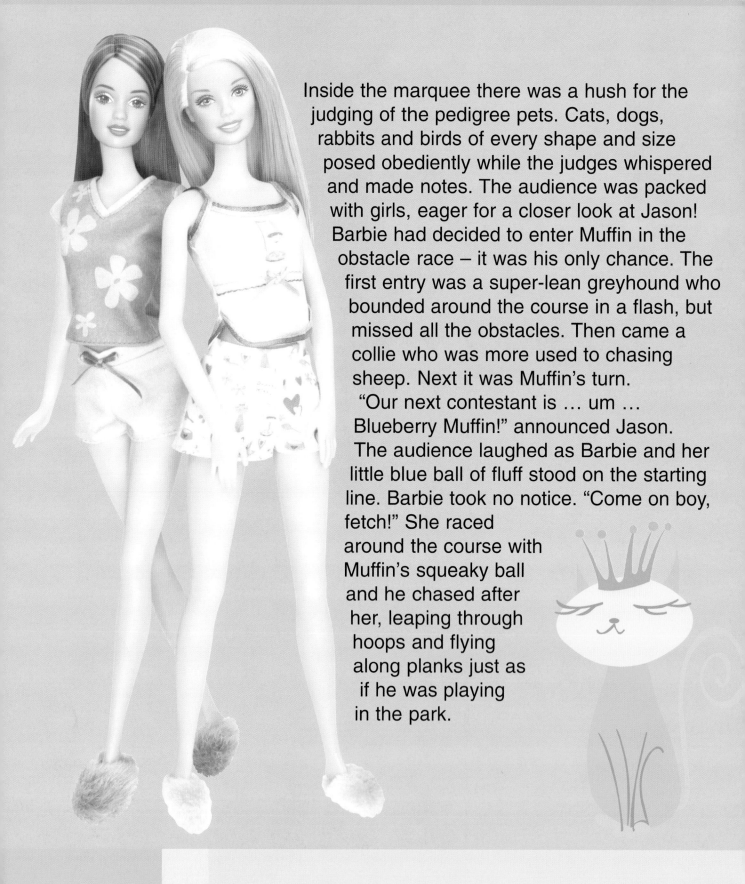

Inside the marquee there was a hush for the judging of the pedigree pets. Cats, dogs, rabbits and birds of every shape and size posed obediently while the judges whispered and made notes. The audience was packed with girls, eager for a closer look at Jason! Barbie had decided to enter Muffin in the obstacle race – it was his only chance. The first entry was a super-lean greyhound who bounded around the course in a flash, but missed all the obstacles. Then came a collie who was more used to chasing sheep. Next it was Muffin's turn.

"Our next contestant is … um … Blueberry Muffin!" announced Jason. The audience laughed as Barbie and her little blue ball of fluff stood on the starting line. Barbie took no notice. "Come on boy, fetch!" She raced around the course with Muffin's squeaky ball and he chased after her, leaping through hoops and flying along planks just as if he was playing in the park.

STORY

The audience was packed with girls, eager for a closer look at Jason!

He yapped and bounced and wagged his tail all the way then skidded round the last bend and crossed the line in record-breaking time! There was a loud cheer.

At the end of the show, Jason stood on the podium to announce the winners.
"Thank you for inviting me here today. I must say Barbie Town is one of the most glamorous places I have visited."
(Gasps and sighs from the audience.) "The Pedigree Pet Cup for the most elegant and perfectly groomed pet in Barbie Town goes to … Persian Princess."
There was an obedient round of applause as Pru accepted the cup.
"But this year I'm happy to present a special prize, on behalf of my TV show. We believe that having a pet is about animals and humans making each other happy. And so the Perfect Pet Cup goes to Muffin, for making everyone laugh!"

"This year I'm happy to present a special prize, on behalf of my TV show."

STORY

41

Pet Puzzles!

a

b   c   d

1   2   3   4

All the girls in Barbie Town love their pets! Can you join these pets to their owners?

Tick the boxes when you find them.

One hairdryer

Two perfume sprays

Three brushes

Four hearts

Five shampoos

Six bones

The Poochie Parlour is a busy place! Can you find all these things in the big picture?

Discover your ideal pet!

1. After school, which do
   you prefer to do?

   a. Play sport
   b. Watch TV
   c. See friends
   d. Use the computer

2. Choose one phrase to
   describe your best friend.

   a. "We both love to do the same things."
   b. "She's someone I can really talk to."
   c. "We laugh and giggle all the time."
   d. "I am my own best friend."

3. What do you like to watch
   best on the TV?

   a. Any kind of sport
   b. A long film
   c. Something funny
   d. A wildlife programme

4. Which pet's name do you prefer?

   a. Scott
   b. Sissy
   c. Sooty
   d. Snip

5. If you were to sponsor a wild
   animal, which would you choose?

   a. Cheetah
   b. Tiger
   c. Koala Bear
   d. Crocodile

6. It's a cold Sunday afternoon.
   Where are you most likely to be?

   a. Out walking in your boots
   b. Inside by the fire
   c. At a friend's house
   d. In your room with a book

Try this quiz, just for fun, and
find out which kind of pet suits you.

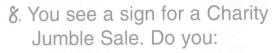

7. Which word best
   describes your bedroom?

   a. Chaotic
   b. Cosy
   c. Chilled
   d. Cosmic

8. You see a sign for a Charity
   Jumble Sale. Do you:

   a. Find out more so that you can
      set up your own stall
   b. Make a note of the date, but
      forget to go
   c. Ignore it – you're bound to be
      too busy
   d. Definitely go – you might find
      something interesting

9. There's a school play coming up.
   Do you:

   a. Sign up as the Director
   b. Offer to help backstage
   c. Audition for a part
   d. Offer to design the
      programmes

Mostly "a"s
Your perfect pet is a dog or
pony! Like you, they are full
of energy and love being
outdoors and having fun.
Your pet would love chasing
through the fields with you!

Mostly "b"s
You are definitely a cat or
rabbit person! You love to be
warm and cosy and would
curl up with your pet for a
cuddle. Purrrrfect!

Mostly "c"s
Your ideal pet is a hamster
or gerbil! Cheeky and funny,
your pet would keep you
amused, and not take up
too much of your time!

Mostly "d"s
You should be the owner of
an interesting insect! You like
to be different and use your
brain. Looking after this pet
would be a challenge to you!

A combination
You are a person with lots of
love to give and plenty of
energy to spare. Any pet
would be lucky to have you
as its owner!

45

Eco Fresh

E46

*It's easy to be green –
as long as you think pink ...*

Barbie was feeling miserable. She had been in bed with a cold for three days. She had missed Teresa's party and now it was raining. She watched the grey raindrops slide down her window. "Everyone's having fun and I'm stuck here," she sighed.

Then the phone rang.

"Hi, Barbie, it's Teresa. Just wanted to say thanks for the present – it's gorgeous! Shall I come over?"

"Don't bother," snapped Barbie. "You might catch my cold." She put the phone down and shuffled out of bed. She moped about her room and then noticed her old toy chest. Her mother must have cleared out the attic. She lifted the lid and found her favourite story book from when she was small, *The Frog Prince*. She snuggled back in bed and began to read …

"Don't bother," snapped Barbie.
"You might catch my cold."

In almost no time she began to feel better. The sun was coming out and Barbie found herself in the garden, fully dressed! She looked around. She had never noticed how beautiful the garden was. She bent down to smell the pink flowers and noticed a pretty pond she never knew existed! Sunlight shimmered on the water and butterflies performed a silent dance. Suddenly she saw a frog, sitting on a rock at the edge of the water. She blinked and pinched herself – she thought she must be dreaming! She looked again. The frog was wearing a crown marked with the letter "J"! "This is not real!" she laughed to herself.

"Thanks!" replied the frog.

"W ... what? A talking frog in my garden – no way! No offence … " she added politely, turning to go back to bed.

"Fine!" he replied. "If I'm not real then you won't want to kiss me to find out if I'm a handsome Prince called James!"

"Oh, for goodness sake," laughed Barbie.

"Don't you believe in magic?" asked the frog.

"I … I do, but not in you!" she replied, and all at once the frog and the pond disappeared.

Barbie shivered. She glanced up and realised she had been standing out in the rain – in her pyjamas! She quickly clambered back up to bed and fell into a deep sleep …

STORY

"A talking frog in my garden - no way!"

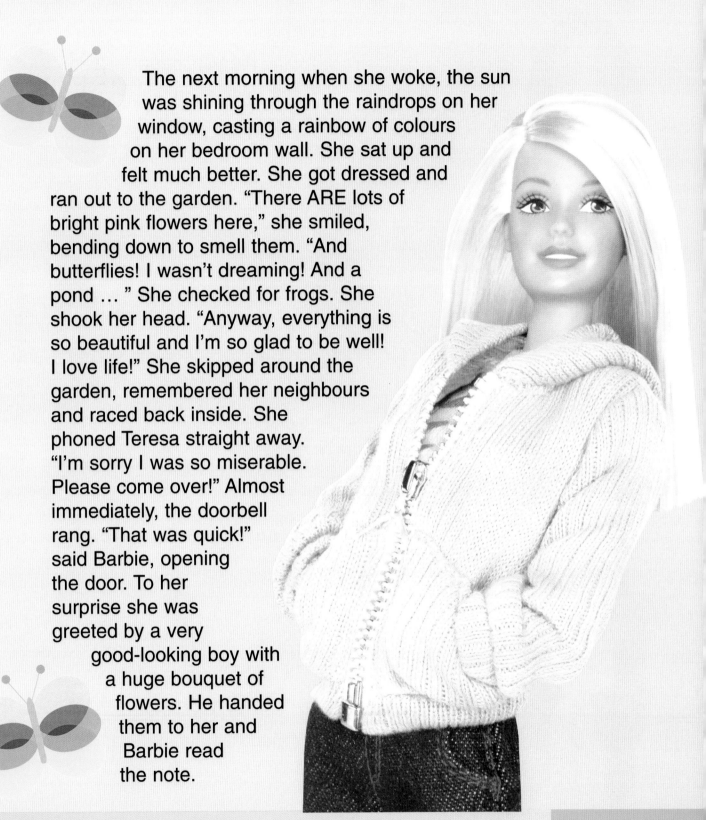

The next morning when she woke, the sun was shining through the raindrops on her window, casting a rainbow of colours on her bedroom wall. She sat up and felt much better. She got dressed and ran out to the garden. "There ARE lots of bright pink flowers here," she smiled, bending down to smell them. "And butterflies! I wasn't dreaming! And a pond … " She checked for frogs. She shook her head. "Anyway, everything is so beautiful and I'm so glad to be well! I love life!" She skipped around the garden, remembered her neighbours and raced back inside. She phoned Teresa straight away. "I'm sorry I was so miserable. Please come over!" Almost immediately, the doorbell rang. "That was quick!" said Barbie, opening the door. To her surprise she was greeted by a very good-looking boy with a huge bouquet of flowers. He handed them to her and Barbie read the note.

"I wasn't dreaming!"

To Barbie,
Please cheer up and
get well soon – we miss you!
Teresa and Kira XXXXX

"Beautiful flowers," said the delivery boy. Then he added, "But not as beautiful as you!"
Barbie blushed.
"Sorry – I don't normally say things like that," he said. "But, well … I'd love to take you out, when you're feeling better. Sorry … let me introduce myself!" He held out his hand. "My name is James … " And round his neck was a necklace, marked with the letter "J".

Later that day, as Barbie prepared for her date, she put *The Frog Prince* back in the chest. "Magic really does happen!" she said, closing the lid. "In fact, magic is everywhere – you just have to remember to look."

STORY

"I'd love to take you out,
when you're feeling better."

Barbie is feeling much better now! Choose
colours to make her look really happy.

51

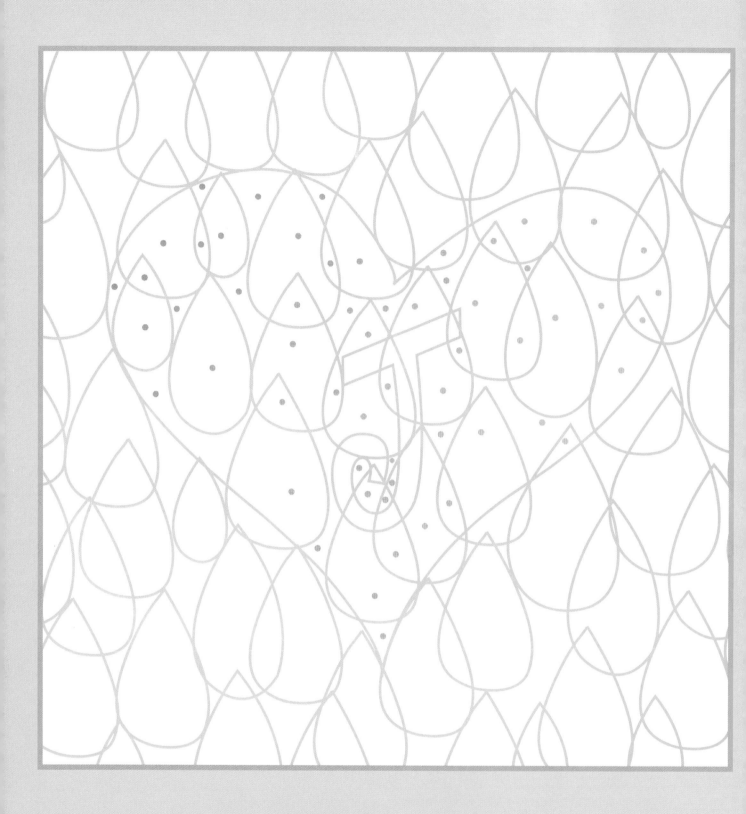

52

Colour the raindrops that are marked with a dot to reveal a special message!

Count the butterflies in the garden.
How many pairs can you find?
Now colour the pairs in matching colours.

Barbie and her friends met up one Friday, after school.

"I hope you'll all come to our Bring and Buy Sale tomorrow," said Kira. "The Brownie Pack is raising money to help endangered animals."

"That's great," said Barbie. "So many beautiful creatures are being wiped out just because humans are so greedy."

"We should do more to help," said Teresa. "We could try to raise money around school."

"We could sell my delicious eco-friendly cakes at break-time … " suggested Kira.

"And I'll make my special super-healthy fruit drinks!" added Barbie. "Be good to your body, and good to the planet!"

"I'll ask Brown Owl if she has any more ideas," said Kira.

STORY

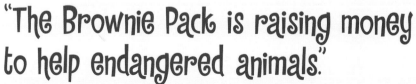
"The Brownie Pack is raising money to help endangered animals."

"Hey," said Barbie, "that reminds me! I heard on the news that owls are becoming really rare! Let's use the owl as our emblem."

"Wise up to save the world!" said Teresa proudly.

"Brilliant!" said Barbie. "I'll design some T-shirts – we could sell them to raise money too."

"And I can make bookmarks with my new printing set," added Kira. "Let's meet up again tomorrow and put our plans into action … "

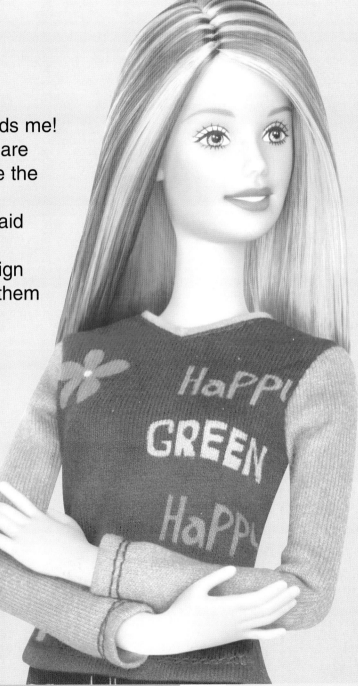

Now turn the page to
see how their ideas look …

Can you think of other ways to help our planet? Write your ideas here, then show them to your friends!

1. ....

2. ....

3. ....

4. ....

5. ....

6. ....

ACTIVITY

Now try to put them into action, just like Barbie!

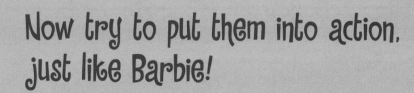

To make four drinks you will need:

    2 bananas
1 orange
4 tablespoons pineapple juice
1 pint milk
4 large scoops vanilla ice cream

Equipment:

    Four tumblers or sundae dishes
Citrus juicer
Mixing bowl
Hand whisk
Ice cream scoop

What to do:

1. Squeeze the juice from the orange
2. Mash the bananas
3. Whisk the mashed bananas, orange and pineapple juices and milk together in the mixing bowl
4. Place a scoop of ice cream in each tumbler and then fill with your fruit mixture

Make the Barbie special super-healthy fruit drinks!

Glamorous Barbie

58

Barbie™

Sometimes, getting ready to go out is more fun than the night itself ...

Help Barbie get ready for a special
night out using your coloured pens.

59

Barbie is preparing for a glamorous night out in Barbie Town ... She has three dresses to choose from, but can you help her pick accessories for each one?

Draw lines to join the things you think Barbie should choose to complete each outfit.

Then colour each dress to help Barbie look her very best!

COLOURING

61

62

Magic is in the air!
So prepare for a fantasy ending ...

Barbie was babysitting for her little sister. She tucked her up in bed, waited until she was quiet, and then told her a story …

Once upon a time there was an enchanted tree. It stood in a forest at the heart of a kingdom ruled by a wise old King. Every autumn, when the moon was round and full, the enchanted tree would sparkle and grant someone's dearest wish.

Now, the wise old King was ill. He had no sons and so he had to choose one of his three daughters to become Queen and rule the kingdom after him. So, when summer turned to autumn and when the moon was round and full, he took his daughters down a secret path to the clearing in the forest where the tree stood, sparkling.

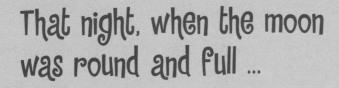

That night, when the moon was round and full …

"My daughters," he began, "I love you all dearly, but only one of you can be Queen. To help me decide, tell me, what is your dearest wish?"
He turned to his eldest daughter first. She was clever, but greedy.

"I wish to marry a wealthy Prince and have the biggest wedding the kingdom has ever seen! I will have jewels and presents galore and the whole kingdom will be rich!"
Then he asked his second daughter, who was beautiful, but vain.

"I wish to be the most adored Queen the kingdom has ever seen! I will dance for the people and enchant them with my grace and beauty."
Finally, he turned to his third daughter, who was good and kind.

"Father, please choose one of my sisters to be Queen. I don't have a taste for jewels. Nor can I enchant our people with dance. My only wish is that you would be well again, because the kingdom will be a sad place without you, and because I love you."

STORY

"To help me decide, tell me, what is your dearest wish?"

The King wiped a tear from his eye, and, as if blown by an invisible wind, the branches of the enchanted tree rustled and a flurry of magic dust lifted on the breeze and settled over the youngest daughter.

Her wish was granted. And, as far as anyone knows, the King rules wisely and justly, to this day.

Barbie looked at her sister. She was fast asleep.
"I hope she didn't miss the ending," whispered Barbie.
"Because sometimes the ending is the best!"

Her wish was granted!

Barbie has two fantasy endings – she just can't decide!

COLOURING

To walk down the aisle as a beautiful bride ...

Help her by colouring
your favourite.

or to wear gowns and
jewels fit for a princess?

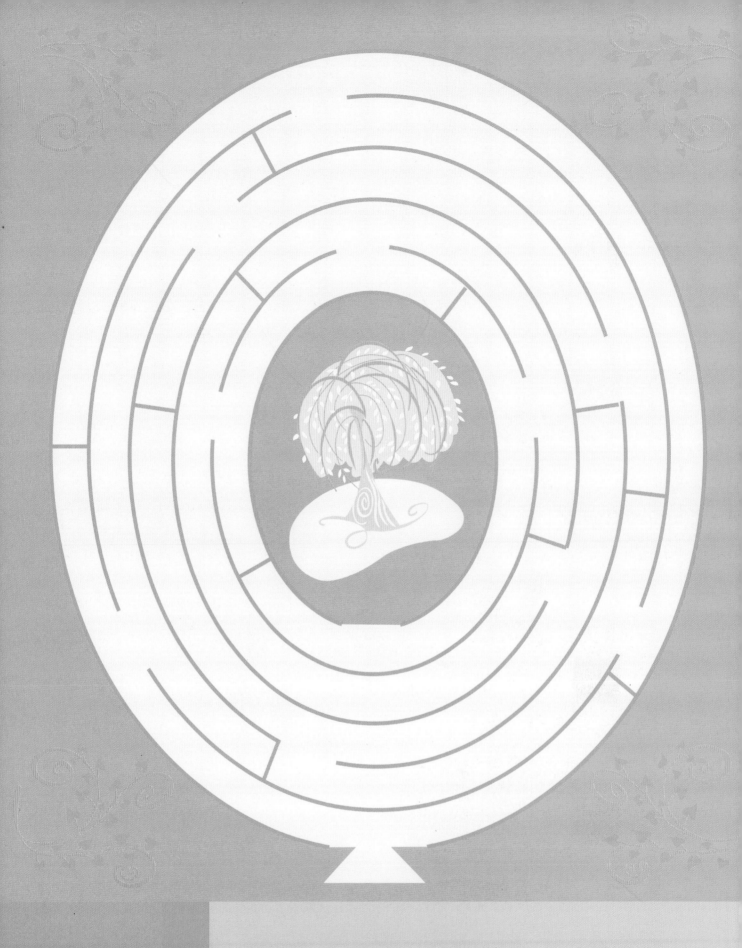

WISH

Find your way along the secret path to
the enchanted tree and make a wish!

Now write your
dearest wish
beneath the
wishing tree.

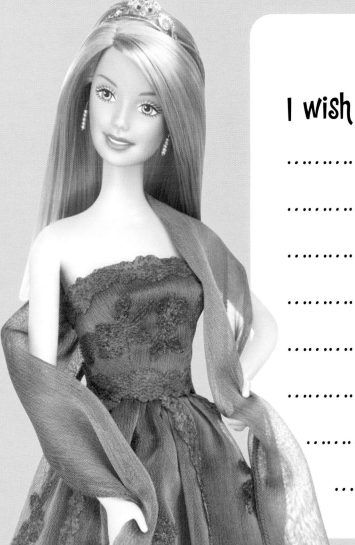

I wish ...

....

....

....

....

....

....

....

....

I hope it comes true!

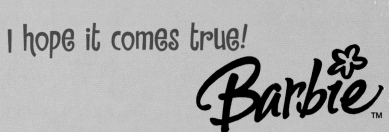